My Weirde

Mr. Nick
Is a
Lunatic!

I'M HUNGRY

Dan Gutman

Pictures by
Jim Paillot

SCHOLASTIC INC.

To Kaden Li

ISBN 978-1-338-17460-1

Text copyright © 2016 by Dan Gutman. Illustrations copyright © 2016 by Jim Paillot.
All rights reserved. Published by Scholastic Inc., 557 Broadway, New York, NY 10012,
by arrangement with HarperCollins Children's Books, a division of
HarperCollins Publishers. SCHOLASTIC and associated logos are
trademarks and/or registered trademarks of Scholastic Inc.

12 11 10 9 8 7 6 5 4 3 2 1   17 18 19 20 21 22

Printed in the U.S.A.   40

First Scholastic printing, February 2017

Typography by Kathleen Duncan

Contents

1. The End of the World   1

2. The Standoff   9

3. Our New Principal   23

4. The *L* Word   35

5. Art Is Like Pulling Teeth   48

6. The Perfect Food   56

7. I Think, Therefore I Am   65

8. Mrs. Hall Is a Goofball   74

9. Release the Dogs!   87

10. Big Surprise Ending   93

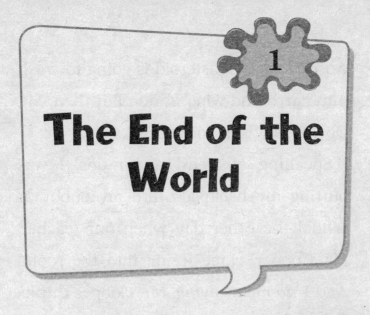

The End of the World

My name is A.J. and I hate it when an asteroid crashes into the earth and wipes out all life on our planet. Don't you hate when that happens?

Our science teacher, Mr. Docker, told us that an asteroid crashed into Earth a million hundred years ago and wiped out the dinosaurs. Ever since then I've been worried that an asteroid is going to crash into Earth and wipe *us* out. But then, Mr. Docker is off his rocker.

Speaking of weird grown-ups, I was putting my backpack into my cubby at school the other day when our teacher, Mr. Cooper, came flying into the room. And I *do* mean *flying*. Mr. Cooper thinks he's a superhero. But he's not a very good one, because he tripped over an umbrella and fell on the garbage can.

"Are you okay?" we all shouted.

"I'm fine," he said, picking the garbage off his pants.

But then something even *weirder* happened. Mr. Cooper grabbed his coat and went flying *out* of the room.

"Gotta run!" he shouted. "Have a nice day!"

WHAT?!

"Aren't we going to pledge the allegiance?" asked my friend Michael, who never ties his shoes.

"Will we have a substitute teacher today?" asked Ryan, who will eat anything, even stuff that isn't food.

"No time to talk!" shouted Mr. Cooper.

And then he was gone.

"*That* was weird," said Neil, who we call the nude kid even though he wears clothes.

"What's weird about it?" asked Andrea Young, this annoying girl with curly brown hair. "Superheroes *always* appear and disappear for no reason."

"Mr. Cooper is probably in a hurry to prevent an asteroid from wiping out all life on Earth," I told everybody. "That's what superheroes do."

"I'm scared," said Emily, who's scared of everything.

"What should we do *now*?" asked Alexia, this girl who rides a skateboard all the time. "We have no teacher."

NO TEACHER?!

I looked at Michael. Michael looked at Ryan. Ryan looked at Neil. Neil looked at me. Then all four of us snapped into action. We got up and shook our butts at the class.

"Boys!" said Andrea, rolling her eyes.

We thought that was the end of it, but you'll never believe who came running through the door at that moment.

Nobody! You can't run through a *door*.

Doors are made of wood. But you'll never believe who ran through the door*way*.

It was two girls from the other third-grade classes.

"Is your teacher gone?" one of the girls asked.

"Yes!" we replied.

"Our teacher is gone too!" the first girl said.

"Our teacher is gone too!" the second girl said.

"Our teacher is gone too!" kids were shouting in the hallway.

In case you were wondering, everybody was shouting that their teacher was gone.

"*All* the teachers are gone!" shouted

Andrea. "Where would they be going first thing in the morning?"

"They must know something we don't know," guessed Alexia.

"The asteroid is on its way!" I shouted.

"The world is about to end!" Ryan shouted.

"Run for your lives!" shouted Neil.

"We've got to *do* something!" shouted Emily, and then she went running out of the room.

Sheesh, get a grip! That girl will fall for *anything.**

---

*Pretty exciting beginning, huh? There's no way we can keep up this pace.

The Standoff

Before we could go running for our lives, I went to the window to see if an asteroid was heading for the earth. What I saw outside was even *weirder*. There was a long line of teachers out there. They were marching up and down the sidewalk. I called everybody over, and we leaned out the window to get a better look.

Mr. Cooper was on the sidewalk. So were our librarian, Mrs. Roopy; our art teacher, Ms. Hannah; and our gym teacher, Miss Small. *All* our teachers were outside, marching back and forth. Even our principal, Mr. Klutz, was out there. He was holding a big sign that said **ON STRIKE**.

"The teachers are on strike!" said

Andrea, as if we couldn't read the sign.

"Mr. Klutz, why are you on strike?" I hollered out the window. "Are you demanding higher pay?"

"No!" yelled Mr. Klutz.

"Are you asking for more vacation time?" asked Andrea.

"No!" yelled Mrs. Roopy.

"Shorter hours?" asked Ryan.

"No!" yelled Ms. Hannah.

"Then why are you on strike?" asked Michael.

"We want coffee!" yelled Mr. Klutz.

Coffee?

Maybe I didn't hear that right.

"What did you say?" I hollered.

"We want coffee!" repeated Mr. Klutz.

"WE WANT COFFEE! WE WANT COFFEE! WE WANT COFFEE!" chanted all the teachers on the sidewalk.

I noticed that some of the other teachers were holding up signs. Our music teacher, Mr. Loring, had a sign that read **I'M A MEANO WITHOUT MY CAPPUCCINO!** Our computer teacher, Mrs. Yonkers, had a sign that read **HECK NO! I NEED A CUP OF JOE!** Our Spanish teacher, Miss Holly, had a sign that read **I WON'T TEACH THE BAMBINOS WITHOUT A FRAPPUCCINO!**

"Two, four, six, eight! What do we appreciate?" the teachers started chanting. "Coffee! Coffee!! *COFFEEEEE!!!*"

Man, grown-ups sure love their coffee. They go a little crazy if they don't have it every morning. That must be the first rule of being a grown-up.

I don't get it. I tried coffee once. It was yucky.

"Don't they have a coffee machine in the teachers' lounge?" asked Neil the nude kid.

That's right. The teachers' lounge is a magical room that has hot tubs, a bowling alley, a helicopter pad, and free back massages. I heard that some first grader snuck in there one time, and he never came out. Nobody knows what happened to him.

"Don't you have a coffee machine in the

teachers' lounge?" Andrea hollered out the window.

"It's broken," shouted the school secretary, Mrs. Patty.

"I bet Mr. Harrison can fix it," hollered Alexia.

Mr. Harrison is the tech guy at our school. His job is to fix the computers, printers, and copy machines when they break down. He can fix anything.

"I tried to fix it!" shouted Mr. Harrison. "The left flange dingle is on the fritz, and the mini–thermal circuit logic board is full of corrosion."

I had no idea what he was talking about.

"We need a *new* coffee machine," Mr.

Klutz shouted, "but the Board of Education won't get us one. So we're on strike."

"I'm bored of education," I said.

"You *always* say that, Arlo," said Andrea, rolling her eyes. She calls me by my real name because she knows I don't like it.

"I always say it because it's always true," I told Andrea.

Outside, the teachers were chanting louder.

"WHAT DO WE WANT?"

"COFFEE!"

"WHEN DO WE WANT IT?"

"NOW!"

That's when the weirdest thing in the history of the world happened. A tank came rolling down the street.

That's right, a *tank*. It was one of those army tanks they have in war movies.

"WOW!" we all said, which is "MOM" upside down.

The tank stopped in the middle of the street, right in front of the teachers. The top of the tank opened up, and you'll never believe in a million hundred years whose head popped out.

It was Dr. Carbles, the president of the Board of Education!

"Where do you think Dr. Carbles got a tank?" Ryan asked.

"From Rent-A-Tank," I told him. "You can rent anything."

Dr. Carbles had a bullhorn in his hand.

"Attention, Ella Mentry School teachers!"

he shouted. "Put down those signs and return to school. I have called in the police and the fire department."

"Will you buy us a new coffee machine?" hollered Mr. Klutz.

"No!" shouted Dr. Carbles. "Go back to work!"

"No brewing? Nothing doing!" shouted Mr. Klutz.

"NO BREWING! NOTHING DOING!" chanted the teachers. "NO BREWING! NOTHING DOING!"

"If you teachers don't return to work right now," shouted Dr. Carbles, "I will be forced to use . . . uh . . . force."

"He's bluffing," said Michael. "Dr. Carbles would never attack our teachers."

The tank started to inch forward. The teachers took a step backward. It was exciting!

And that's when the most amazing thing in the history of the world happened. Mr. Klutz went over and stood right in front of the tank!

He put his hand in the air.

The tank stopped.

"Move out of the way, Klutz!" shouted Dr. Carbles. "I'm warning you. I will crush your rebellion!"

"No!" Mr. Klutz shouted back. "I'm not moving until you buy us a new coffee machine for the teachers' lounge."

"Mr. Klutz is *so* brave," Andrea said. "When I grow up, I want to be just like him."

"He's my hero," said Emily, who always agrees with everything Andrea says.

At that moment we heard sirens coming down the street. A bunch of police cars and fire trucks pulled up and screeched to a halt.

"I'll give you *one* last chance, Klutz," shouted Dr. Carbles. "Go back to school now, or else!"

"Not until we get a new coffee machine!" Mr. Klutz shouted back.

"Okay, you asked for it, Klutz!" shouted Dr. Carbles. "Turn on the water hoses, men! Release the dogs!"*

---

*How come this book is called *Mr. Nick Is a Lunatic!* and there's nobody named Mr. Nick? That's weird.

Our New Principal

A bunch of firefighters jumped off the fire truck with hoses, and they started spraying water at Mr. Klutz and our teachers. The teachers were yelling and screaming and shrieking and hooting and hollering and freaking out. Then a bunch of dogs jumped out of the police cars and started barking and chasing the teachers down the street!

Did you ever see that movie *Ratatouille*? This was like that scene when the people come in the kitchen, and the rats scatter in all directions. You should have been there! It was hilarious. And we got to see it with our own eyes!

Well, it's pretty hard to see stuff with somebody else's eyes.

"Ooh, I don't like to see this," said Andrea, shaking her head. "I don't like violence."

"What do you have against violins?" I asked.

"Not violins, Arlo! Violence!"

I knew that. I was just yanking Andrea's chain.

In a few minutes Mr. Klutz and the teachers were gone. The firefighters packed up their hoses. The policemen rounded up the dogs and left.

"That will teach them to rebel against me," Dr. Carbles said. "My work is done here."

Then he closed the hatch and drove the tank away.

Dr. Carbles is losing his marbles.

"Well, *that* was weird," I said.

"What are we supposed to do *now*?" asked Alexia. "Should we just go home?"

Hmmm. All the teachers were gone. There was no point in shaking our butts at the class, because we already did that. There was nothing to prevent us from leaving school.

No more school! And it wasn't even a snow day. This was the greatest moment of my life!

"NO MORE SCHOOL!" I chanted. "NO MORE SCHOOL! NO MORE SCHOOL!"

I figured *everybody* was going to start chanting "No more school!" with me.

I looked around. Nobody else was chanting. Everybody was just looking at me.

I hate when that happens.

That's when the weirdest thing in the history of the world happened. A yellow bus pulled up outside the school.

Well, that's not the weird part, because yellow buses pull up outside our school all the time. The weird part was what happened next.

A bunch of grown-ups got out of the yellow bus. The first one was a tall guy with really long hair. He had a bullhorn, just like the one Dr. Carbles was carrying. I guess grown-ups really like talking into bullhorns.

"Yo!" the tall guy hollered up at us. "To all you students looking out the windows. My name is Mr. Nick. I will be the replacement principal while Mr. Klutz and your teachers are on strike. Everybody, please report to the all-porpoise room."

The all-*porpoise* room?

"Don't you mean the all-purpose room?" somebody shouted.

"Oh, yeah," Mr. Nick hollered. "Please report to the all-purpose room."

That was weird. There's no such thing as an all-porpoise

28

room. How would we be able to use the room if it was filled with porpoises? And why would porpoises come to school in the first place? Don't they need to live in water? Who would feed them? I've heard of schools of fish, but this is ridiculous.

There was no time to worry about porpoises. We walked a million hundred miles to the other side of the school. Even though we didn't have a teacher, we went in single file anyway. Neil was the line leader. Alexia was the door holder.

When we got to the all-purpose room, Mr. Nick and a bunch of other people were up on the stage. After all the kids were seated, he made a peace sign with his fingers. In our school a peace sign means "shut up."

Everybody stopped talking.

"Hey, how come you all stopped talking?" asked Mr. Nick.

"You made the shut-up peace sign," I yelled.

"No, that was a *real* peace sign," Mr. Nick said, holding up his fingers again. "I just wanted to say peace, man. Everybody chill. If we could just have more peace in the world, we wouldn't have so many problems like this. The world would be a better place. Can you dig where I'm coming from?"

I can dig, but I had no idea where he was

coming from. So I didn't know where he wanted us to dig. Mr. Nick talked funny.

"When will our regular teachers be coming back?" somebody shouted from the back of the room.

"My staff and I will be here for at least a week," Mr. Nick said, "or until the strike is over. Any other questions?"

Little Miss Perfect was waving her hand in the air like she was trying to hail a taxi. So of course Mr. Nick called on her.

"You're a grown-up," Andrea said. "Don't *you* need to drink coffee in the morning like our regular teachers do?"

"No, man," Mr. Nick replied. "That stuff will mess with your body. I drink in the sunshine, baby! That's *my* caffeine. Mr. Klutz and your old teachers need to mellow out, man. They drink too much coffee. That's why they're so uptight all the time."

Huh! I always wondered why all the teachers at our school were so weird. Now I knew the truth: it was all that coffee they drank every morning!

"From now on we're gonna do things differently at Ella Mentry School," said Mr. Nick. "If you want to learn stuff, that's cool. And if you don't want to learn stuff, that's cool too. We go with the flow. If you want to stare out the window and just groove on the vibes, that's cool. Different strokes for different folks. No more pencils. No more books. No more teacher's dirty looks. Right? No more rules. That's my attitude, man."

Wow, Mr. Nick sounded like a cool guy!

Andrea had on her mean face, and I knew why. She *loves* pencils and books and teachers and rules and learning stuff.

"I think rules are a *good* thing," she

said. "If people don't follow the rules, you end up with chaos."

I didn't know what chaos was, but it didn't sound like a good thing.

"Well, I do have *one* rule," announced Mr. Nick. "You all have to go back to your classrooms now and meet your new teachers."

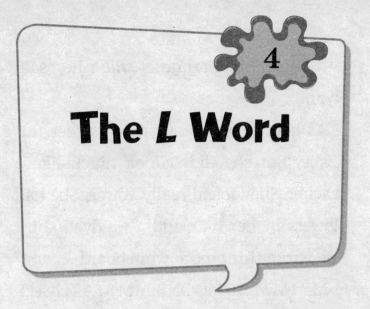

The *L* Word

We walked a million hundred miles back to our classroom. Everybody was excited to see who our new teacher would be.

"I hope she's nice," said Emily, who always hopes everybody will be nice.

"She might not be a *she*," said Andrea. "Maybe she will be a *he*. Mr. Cooper is a he. Our old teacher Mr. Granite was a he."

"I think Mr. Granite is *still* a he," said Ryan.

As it turned out, our new teacher *was* a she. But she didn't look much like a teacher. She looked really young. She had flowers in her hair and a tie-dyed shirt. She wrote this on the whiteboard . . .

MY NAME IS MOONBEAM STARLIGHT.

Huh? What kind of a name is Moonbeam Starlight?

"You can call me Miss Moon," she told us as we took our seats. "I'm Mr. Nick's girlfriend."

"Are you a teacher too?" asked Alexia.

"Aren't we *all* teachers?" Miss Moon replied with a smile.

"Where do you live?" asked Neil.

"Mr. Nick and I live in a yurt," said Miss Moon. "Does anybody know what a yurt is?"

I raised my hand. Miss Moon called on me.

"A yurt is 'yogurt' without the *OG* in it," I said.

Everybody laughed even though I didn't say anything funny.

Andrea was waving her hand in the air like she was cleaning a big window. Miss Moon called on her.

"A yurt is a big, round tent," Andrea said.

"That's right, Andrea!"

Andrea smiled the smile she smiles to let everybody know she knows something nobody else knows. She probably looked up "yurt" on her smartphone. What is her problem? Why can't a truck full of yurts fall on her head?

"Mr. Nick and I live off the grid, and we grow wildflowers," said Miss Moon.

"We're planning to open up a vegetarian bookstore."

"How is a vegetarian bookstore different from a regular bookstore?" Michael asked.

"Our books will have no meat in them," said Miss Moon.

That was weird. I never heard of a book with meat in it. Why would anybody put meat in a book? Well, maybe if it was a book about meat.

Miss Moon closed her eyes and began dancing around the front of the class.

"Are you going to teach us reading today?" asked Andrea.

"No," said Miss Moon. "What's the point

of teaching you reading? You already know how to read, don't you?"

"Well, yes," replied Andrea. "Are you going to teach us writing?"

"No," said Miss Moon. "You already know how to write, don't you?"

"I guess so," replied Andrea. "So, are you going to teach us math?"

"No," said Miss Moon. "You already know how to do math, don't you?"

"Uh, yes," replied Andrea. "Then what *are* you going to teach us?"

Miss Moon went to the cloakroom and took out a guitar.

"I'm going to teach you how to *love*," she said.

WHAT?! Ugh, disgusting! She said the *L* word! I thought I was gonna throw up.

Miss Moon strummed the guitar.

"Let's sing a love song," she said. "I think you'll pick up the words very quickly."

And then she began to sing this really weird song. It went something like this. . . .

"Love, love . . ."

Ugh! Miss Moon's dumb song was nothing but the *L* word over and over again! I thought I was gonna die. It was also the most boring song in the history of the world. What a snoozefest!

I never thought I would ever say this, but I was wishing we could learn reading, writing, or math instead of listening to Miss Moon sing.

Finally, Miss Moon finished her awful song and put down the guitar. Everybody clapped, because that's what you're supposed to do when somebody finishes singing a song, no matter how horrible it is. Miss Moon picked up some papers and put a sheet on everybody's desk.

"Okay," she said. "Now that we're all in a loving mood, I'd like you to write something that you love about the person sitting to your left."

I looked to my left. And you'll never believe in a million hundred years who was sitting there.

It was Andrea! She looked at me. She had a big smile on her face.

I turned around. Ryan and Michael were elbowing each other and pointing at me. They had big smiles on their faces too.

Oh no! I had to write something I love about Andrea! This was the worst day in the history of the world.

I didn't know what to say. I didn't know what to do. I had to think fast. So this is what I wrote. . . .

I LOVE IT WHEN ANDREA IS ABSENT.

I figured Miss Moon was going to collect all the papers and take them back to her yurt to read. But no such luck.

"Okay," she said. "Now we're going to read what we wrote out loud in front of the class. Who wants to go first?"

"A.J. wants to go first!" shouted Michael.

"A.J. wants to go first!" shouted Ryan.

"A.J. wants to go first!" shouted Neil.

In case you were wondering, all the guys were shouting that I wanted to go first.

"How about you go first, A.J.?" said Miss Moon.

Bummer in the summer! I thought I was gonna die. This was the worst thing to happen since TV Turnoff Week! I wanted to go run away to Antarctica and live with the penguins.

I stood up. Michael and Ryan were covering their mouths and giggling.

"I love it when Andrea is absent," I muttered under my breath.

"I'm sorry," said Miss Moon. "Can you

speak a little louder, A.J.?"

"I love it when Andrea is absent," I said
a little louder.

"That's mean, Arlo!" said Andrea.

"*Oooooh!*" Ryan said. "A.J. loves something about Andrea!"

"When are you gonna get married?" asked Michael.

If those guys weren't my best friends, I would hate them.

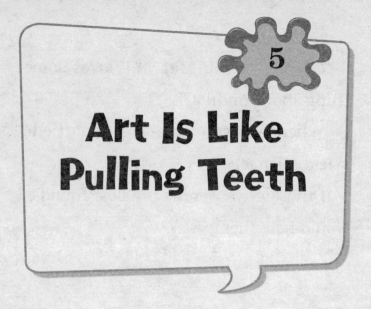

Art Is Like
Pulling Teeth

After Miss Moon had totally humiliated me in front of the whole class, she said it was time for us to go to art. Ugh! Art is boring. We had to walk a million hundred miles to the art room.

Our regular art teacher, Ms. Hannah, wasn't there, of course. She was on strike.

Instead, some man was in the art room. He was wearing one of those white smock thingies and carrying a box.

"Hi, I'm Mr. Bob," he told us after we had taken our seats. "Art is blah blah blah blah creativity blah blah blah blah blah blah imagination blah blah blah blah color blah blah blah blah expression blah blah blah blah . . ."

I had no idea what Mr. Bob was talking about. But he seemed to know a lot of stuff about art.

"Do you kids like art?" he asked us.

"Yes!" said all the girls.

"No!" said all the boys.

"Would you like to draw some pictures?"

"Yes!" said all the girls.

"No!" said all the boys.

Mr. Bob opened the box he was carrying and took a bunch of hand mirrors out of it. He went around the room passing out one mirror to each of us.

"Today we're going to draw self-portraits," Mr. Bob told us. "A self-portrait is a picture of yourself. We're going to make self-portraits of the insides of our mouths."

WHAT?!

"You want us to draw pictures of our *mouths*?" asked Alexia.

"Yes! The mouth is an amazing part of the body," said Mr. Bob. "Think about it.

We use our mouth for eating, for speaking, for kissing—"

"Ewwwww, gross!" everybody shouted.

"—and sometimes we even breathe through our mouth. Yet we hardly ever look *inside* our mouth. We sure are lucky we have one. I don't know where I would be without my mouth."

I know where Mr. Bob would be. In a loony bin! Mr. Bob is a nut job.

"I don't want to draw a picture of my mouth," I said while he was passing out paper and pencils.

"Getting kids to draw is like pulling teeth," said Mr. Bob. "I'll tell you what, A.J. I'll draw the inside of your mouth *for* you."

Before I could make a run for the door, Mr. Bob had leaned me back in my chair and was looking into my mouth.

"Open wide," he said. "Say *Ahhhh*."

I opened my mouth wide and said *Ahhhh*.

"You really need to floss more," he told me. "I think there may be a few cavities in here."

"Ahrgrahbahrahrgabrar," I said, because Mr. Bob's fingers were in my mouth.

He started drawing a picture of the inside of my mouth. It was actually pretty good. Everybody else in the class was drawing their own mouth pictures.

Finally, after a million hundred hours, the torture was over. Mr. Bob told us to hold up our drawings.

"Nice work!" he said. "You kids are really talented mouth artists."

Miss Moon came back into the classroom. She said she *loved* our mouth drawings and told us to line up because it was time to go to lunch. Mr. Bob said good-bye to each of us as we left.

"Catch you next time," he said.

"You're not really an art teacher, are you?" I whispered to him.

"Of course not," he replied. "I never said I was an art teacher."

"Then who *are* you?" I asked.

"I'm Mr. Nick's dentist."

WHAT?!

"Oh, yeah," Mr. Bob told me. "I've been

friends with Nick since we were in high school together. He called me up this morning and asked me to come over here and teach art this week. I would do anything for that guy."

And I thought our *old* teachers were weird!

The Perfect Food

We eat lunch in the vomitorium. It used to be called the cafetorium, but then some first grader threw up in there. I usually bring my lunch from home, but my mom forgot to pack it, so I had to buy lunch.

"Something tells me that Mr. Nick is not a real principal," I said as I waited on line with the guys.

"What do you mean, A.J.?" asked Ryan.

"Well, Mr. Bob told me he isn't a real art teacher," I explained. "He's just Mr. Nick's dentist. And Miss Moon isn't a real teacher. So maybe Mr. Nick isn't a real principal either. Real principals have lots of rules, and real principals don't call the all-purpose room the all-porpoise room."

"Mr. Nick must be . . . an imposter!" said Michael.

"Yeah," said Neil. "He probably tied up Mr. Klutz to some railroad tracks, and a train is about to run him over. Stuff like that happens all the time."

"We've got to *do* something!" shouted Emily. And then she went running out of the vomitorium.

I slapped my forehead. What a crybaby!

Finally, after we waited for a million hundred minutes, we got up to the front of the line. There was a lady behind the counter. I had never seen her before.

"Where's Ms. LaGrange, our regular lunch lady?" Ryan asked her.

"She's on strike with all the teachers," the lady said. "My name is Miss Julia."

"You're not a *real* cook, are you?" asked Alexia.

"Of *course* I'm a real cook," said Miss Julia. "In fact, I'm Mr. Nick's personal cook and nutrition adviser."

Oh no. I didn't like the sound of that.

"What would you kids like to eat for

lunch today?" asked Miss Julia. "You can have anything you want."

"I'll have a hot dog," I said.

"I'll have chicken fingers," said Andrea.

"I'll have a hamburger," said Alexia.

"Sorry," Miss Julia told us. "I don't eat meat, and I don't serve meat."

"You're a vegetarian?" Michael asked.

"No," said Miss Julia. "I don't eat vegetables either, and I won't serve them."

"How about eggs?" Ryan asked. "Do you eat eggs?"

"Eggs?! Are you crazy?" said Miss Julia. "Do you have any idea what they do to the chickens that lay those eggs?"

"Milk? Cheese?" I asked hopefully.

"Please! Dairy?" said Miss Julia. "No *way*! It's out of the question."

"Seafood?" asked Andrea. "Could I have some tuna fish, please?"

"Nope," said Miss Julia. "Tuna is full of mercury and other chemicals."

"Can I just have a piece of bread?" asked Alexia. "I'm really hungry."

"Sorry. This is a gluten-free school now. No bread."

"So what *can* we have for lunch?" I asked. "You said we could have anything we want."

"Aha!" said Miss Julia. "You're in luck. Today we are serving some delicious, organic, gluten-free, all-natural, free-range water. With no preservatives."

Wait. WHAT?!

"You're giving us glasses of water for *lunch*?" I asked.

"Of course not!" said Miss Julia. "Don't be silly. I boiled the water to kill the germs.

Here, you can each have a bowl of water soup."

Water soup?

Miss Julia handed a bowl of water to each of us. The bowls were hot, and steam was coming out of them.

"Water soup? Is this some kind of a joke?" asked Ryan, who will eat anything.

Ryan totally doesn't know what a joke is. A joke would be like: What kind of flowers are on your face? Tulips!

"Water is the liquid of life," Miss Julia told us. "Think about it. Water has no calories. No sugar. No artificial ingredients. No sodium. No cholesterol. No GMOs. It's the perfect food. Drink up! You'll feel better."

I *knew* I should have brought my lunch from home. We took our bowls of water soup and sat down at a table.

Miss Julia is peculiar.*

---

*Thanks to Monty Python for "The Cheese Shop" sketch. YouTube it!

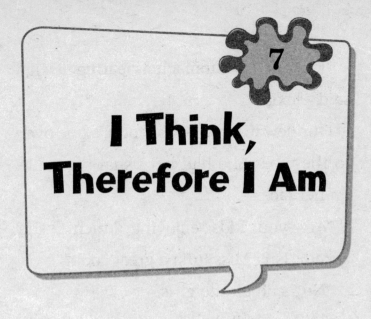

I Think, Therefore I Am

7

"This soup is pretty watery," I said as I sipped from my bowl of water soup.

"I'm hungry," said Neil.

"Me too," said Michael.

"I'm starving," said Ryan. "I would eat *anything* right now."

"You'll eat anything *anytime,*" I told him. "Even stuff that isn't food."

"I think my stomach is eating itself," said Alexia.

Our new teacher, Miss Moon, came over to the table. She had her usual big smile on her face.

"Are you kids enjoying lunch?" she asked. "Isn't Miss Julia a great cook?"

"No," said all the girls.

"No," said all the boys.

Miss Moon led us back to our classroom. She said it was time for math. Ugh. Math is boring.

"I thought you said you weren't going to teach us math," said Andrea.

"I'm *not* going to teach you math," said Miss Moon. "Mr. Nick is bringing in a special teacher to teach you math."

And you'll never believe in a million hundred years who walked into the door at that moment.

Nobody! It would hurt to walk into a door. I thought we went over that in chapter one. But you'll never believe who walked into the door*way*.

It was Mr. Nick!

"*You're* the special math teacher?" I asked.

"Yeah, I dig math," said Mr. Nick. "Numbers are my bag, dude."

Oh no. I had a bad feeling about this.

"Let's start with the basics to see how much you kids know about math," said Mr. Nick. "Can anybody tell me what you get when you add two plus two?"

Andrea looked like she was going to burst. She was waving her hand in the air like she was stranded on a desert island and had to signal an airplane.

"You don't have to raise your hands anymore," Mr. Nick told us. "We have no rules here, remember? So, Andrea, what is two plus two?"

"Four!" she shouted. Then she smiled the smile that she smiles to let everybody know she got the right answer.

Mr. Nick closed his eyes and stroked his chin for a minute.

"Hmmm," he said. "That is a very interesting answer, Andrea. But what if two plus two *isn't* four?"

WHAT?!

"But of *course* two plus two is four," Andrea told him. "Everybody knows that. I don't even have to look it up."

Mr. Nick looked around like he didn't want anybody else to hear. Then he lowered his voice to a whisper.

"Your teachers have been telling you all your life that two plus two is four," he whispered, "but what if two plus two is actually five?"

Here we go.

"What if *everything* your teachers ever taught you is wrong?" Mr. Nick whispered. "Maybe you've been brainwashed your whole life. Did you ever think about that?"

"B-but I *know* that two plus two is four," Andrea said as she took some pencils out of her pencil case. "Look, if I put two pencils on my desk, and then I put two *more* pencils on my desk, and then I count the pencils, it comes to four pencils. One . . . two . . . three . . . four."

Andrea was right, for once in her life.

"Well, you're entitled to your opinion, Andrea," said Mr. Nick. "This is a free country. Our Founding Fathers gave us freedom of speech. But if you ask me, numbers are a state of mind. Maybe everybody is wrong, and two plus two is actually sixty-five. Maybe it's *minus* four. Maybe in another universe two plus two is a *billion* and four. Doesn't that blow your mind?"

"But . . . but . . . but . . ."

We all started giggling because Andrea said "but," which sounds just like "butt" even though it only has one *T.* Then Andrea put on her mean face.

"That's crazy!" she said. "Two plus two is four, and that's all there is to it!"

"Hey, chill, girl," Mr. Nick said, flashing

a peace sign. "Let's try to be tolerant of people who don't agree with our opinions. Haters gonna hate, but we don't have to be close-minded. Let's be accepting of all views. I say, let's teach the controversy."

I didn't know what he was talking about. Mr. Nick is a lunatic!

"Okay, I think that's enough math for today," Mr. Nick said. "The point of this lesson is, are you gonna think for yourself? Or are you going to let The Man tell you what to think?"

I looked around. The only man in the room was Mr. Nick.

"Remember the words of the great French mathematician Descartes," Mr.

Nick said as he walked out the door. "I think, therefore I am."

I think, therefore I am? That made no sense at all. I am what I am, even if I don't think about who I am. That guy Descartes was weird.

I don't care *what* Mr. Nick says. Two plus two is definitely four.

I think.

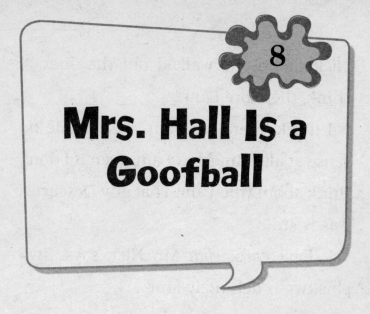

Mrs. Hall Is a Goofball

It was one o'clock in the afternoon. Or maybe it was two o'clock. I'm not sure. I was so hungry that I couldn't think straight. All I had for lunch was a bowl of water soup.

As soon as Mr. Nick left, some lady came into our classroom. I had never seen her before.

"My name is Mrs. Hall," she said. "I'm here to teach you creative writing."

"I'll bet you're not even a creative writing teacher," said Ryan.

"You're right, I'm not," said Mrs. Hall. "I'm Mr. Nick's yoga instructor. But how hard could it be to teach creative writing? You just put words on a page, right?"

"Ooh, can we write a story?" asked Andrea. "I love stories!"

"Me too!" said Emily, who always agrees with everything Andrea says. The two of them were all excited.

"You can create anything you want," said Mrs. Hall as she handed out sheets of paper to all of us. "That's why it's called *creative* writing."

"I'm going to write a story about butter-flies," said Andrea.

"Me too!" said Emily.

The two of them started writing on their papers.

Writing is boring. I didn't know what to write. I didn't feel like being creative. I felt like eating.

I looked around. Everybody else had already started writing stuff on their papers. Mrs. Hall was looking at me.

"How about you, A.J.?" she asked. "What do you want to write about?"

"I don't know," I admitted. "I don't have any ideas."

"*Everybody* has ideas," she replied. "What do you *care* about? What's *important* to you? What are you *passionate* about?"

I thought and thought and thought. I thought so hard that my brain hurt. I thought so hard that I thought my head was going to explode. Or maybe I was just hungry.

That's it! I took a crayon out of my desk and wrote this in big letters. . . .

I'M HUNGRY.

"Good, A.J.!" said Mrs. Hall. "I like the passion you put into that! You get an A in creative writing."

Ha! I wrote two words on a piece of paper and I got an A? Not bad! Hey, creative writing isn't so terrible after all.

Andrea looked up from her desk. She had on her mean face.

"That's not fair!" she complained. "Arlo just wrote 'I'm hungry,' and he got an A for creative writing? I was going to write a ten-page story about butterflies."

Ha! Nah-nah-nah boo-boo on Andrea.

"You can create whatever you want," said Mrs. Hall. "It doesn't matter how long your story is. As long as you write what you feel passionate about."

Andrea turned over her sheet of paper. Then she wrote this on the other side. . . .

I WANT MR. COOPER BACK.

"*That's* what I feel passionate about," she said.

"Good, Andrea!" said Mrs. Hall. "You get an A in creative writing too."

"That's not fair!" I complained. "Andrea stole my idea. I was creative before she was creative!"

"*Anybody* can write whatever they want," said Mrs. Hall. "It doesn't matter who did it first."

Everybody in the class saw that Andrea and I had gotten As for doing nothing. They all turned over their sheets of paper and started writing like crazy on the other side with crayons.

Alexia wrote I WANT TO LEARN SOMETHING on her paper.

Michael wrote THIS SCHOOL IS MESSED UP.

Emily wrote I WANT MR. COOPER BACK TOO.

Ryan wrote MR. NICK IS A LUNATIC.

Neil wrote THESE TEACHERS ARE FAKES.

"Yes! Yes!" said Mrs. Hall. "I like your passion! Express yourselves! Let it flow! You kids are so creative!"

Mrs. Hall said we all got As for creative writing and that we should keep working. She excused herself and said she had to go to the ladies' room.

"I can't believe she gave us all As," said Ryan as soon as Mrs. Hall left. "I just wrote five words."

"This class is bogus," said Michael.

"This whole *school* is bogus," said Alexia.

"Yeah," everybody agreed.

"Hey, we should go on strike," I suggested. "We should go march around outside with these signs like our real teachers did."

Everybody looked at me for a minute.

"That would be *cool*!" Ryan finally said.

"A.J., you're a genius!" said Alexia.

"Let's do it!" said Andrea. Even *she* liked my idea.

I should get the Nobel Prize. That's a prize they give out to people who don't have bells.

"I'm scared," said Emily. "We could get in trouble."

"Let's go!" I shouted.

We all picked up our signs and rushed out of the classroom. We didn't even go quietly in single file. There was no line leader. No door holder.

It's cool having no rules! We just ran a million hundred miles down the hall until we got to the front door.

That's when Mr. Nick came running out of the principal's office.

"Hey, where are you kids going?" he shouted. "It's not time for dismissal yet."

"We're expressing our creativity!" I yelled back at him. Then I flashed him a peace sign.

"That's right," yelled Andrea. "We're not going to let The Man tell us what to do! We're thinking for ourselves."

"Come back here, you kids!" Mr. Nick

shouted. But it was too late. We were already out the door.

On the sidewalk, we all started marching, shouting, and holding up our signs. It was cool. Creative writing is fun.

"WE WANT OUR TEACHERS BACK!"

we chanted. "WE WANT OUR TEACHERS BACK!"

A few minutes later the front door opened, and a bunch of kids from the other classes came running outside. I guess they saw us out the window. Some

of them were carrying signs of their own.

"Join us!" Andrea shouted to them. "We're on strike!"

"WE'RE ON STRIKE!" we all chanted. "WE'RE ON STRIKE!"

That's when the weirdest thing in the history of the world happened. But I'm not going to tell you what it was.

Okay, okay, I'll tell you.

A tank came rolling down the street.

Release the Dogs!

The tank stopped in the middle of the street, right in front of us. The hatch on the top opened up, and I think you can guess whose head popped out. It was Dr. Carbles, the president of the Board of Education, of course.

"What are you kids doing out of school?" he asked.

"WE WANT OUR TEACHERS BACK!" we chanted. "WE WANT OUR TEACHERS BACK!"

"Put down those silly signs and return to class," Dr. Carbles shouted through a bullhorn. "I have called in the police and the fire department."

"Will you bring back our old teachers?" asked Andrea.

"No!" shouted Dr. Carbles. "Go back to school!"

"WE WANT OUR TEACHERS! NOT SOME WEIRD CREATURES!" somebody shouted.

"WE WANT OUR TEACHERS! NOT SOME WEIRD CREATURES!" we all started chanting.

"If you kids don't return to school *right now*," shouted Dr. Carbles, "I will be forced to turn on the hoses and release the dogs."

"Dogs?" I said. "I *love* dogs!"

I do love dogs. And getting sprayed by hoses is fun. One time I was washing my dog, Buttons, with a hose and all the neighbors came over with their dogs, and we had a big neighborhood dog-washing party. Everybody was spraying each other with water. That was cool.

"Dr. Carbles has *attack* dogs, dumbhead!" said Andrea. "He's going to *attack* us with dogs and hoses!"

"Your *face* looks like an attack dog," I told Andrea, because I couldn't think of anything else to say.

"Oh, snap!" said Ryan.

"He's bluffing," said Michael. "Dr. Carbles would never attack a bunch of kids with dogs."

"Oh, you don't think so?" shouted Dr. Carbles.

The tank started to inch forward.

We all took a step backward.

That's when the most amazing thing in the history of the world happened. Andrea went over and stood right in front of the tank. She put her hand in the air.

The tank stopped moving.

"Move out of the way, young lady!" shouted Dr. Carbles. "I'm warning you. I will crush your rebellion, just like I crushed your teachers' rebellion!"

"No!" Andrea shouted back. "I'm not moving until our teachers are allowed to come back to school."

"Andrea is *so* brave," Emily said. "When I grow up, I want to be just like Andrea."

At that moment sirens started blaring down the street. A bunch of police cars and fire trucks pulled up and screeched to a halt.

"I'll give you *one* last chance, Andrea," shouted Dr. Carbles. "Go back to school right now, or else!"

"Not until our teachers come back!" Andrea shouted.

"Okay, you asked for it!" shouted Dr. Carbles. "Turn on the water hoses, men! Release the dogs!"*

---

*Isn't this exciting? Aren't you glad you're reading this instead of one of those boring Newbery books?

Big Surprise Ending

I have to tell you, there was electricity in the air.

Well, not really. If there was electricity in the air, we would have all been electrocuted.

Before Dr. Carbles and his men had the chance to attack us, the weirdest thing in the history of the world happened. A deliveryman came walking up the street.

Well, that's not the weird part, because deliverymen come walking up the street every day. The weird part was what happened next.

"Howdy-do, everybody," the deliveryman said. "What's all the ruckus about? I have a package here for Ella Mentry School."

"Put that box down!" shouted Mr. Nick as he came running out of the school. "There might be a bomb in there."

"A bomb!"

"A bomb?"

"A bomb!!"

In case you were wondering, everybody was saying "a bomb." The deliveryman put the big box on the sidewalk very gently.

A policeman got out of his car with one of the dogs. The dog started sniffing around the box.

"She's trained to sniff out bombs," said the policeman.

"Maybe there's some food in that box," Ryan whispered to me. "I'm starving."

The dog stopped sniffing. I guess there wasn't a bomb in the box.

Mr. Nick went over to the box and got down on his hands and knees. He slowly tore off a piece of tape on the top of the box.

"Stand clear," he said. "There could be *anything* in this package."

It was so exciting! There was electricity

in the air. Well, not really. I thought we went over that already. But we were on pins and needles.

Well, not really. We were just standing there. If we were on pins and needles, it would have hurt. But we were all glued to our seats.

Well, not exactly. That would be weird. And there were no chairs outside. Why would anybody glue themselves to a seat anyway? How would you get the glue off?

Mr. Nick opened the flaps on the box.

He reached inside.

He pulled something out. It was big.

We all moved closer to get a better look.

"It's a . . . coffee machine!" Mr. Nick said.

"Who ordered that?" shouted Dr. Carbles angrily. "I didn't buy a coffee machine."

"No, but *we* did!"

We all turned around. And you'll never believe in a million hundred years who was standing there. I'm not going to tell you.

Okay, okay, I'll tell you.

It was Mr. Klutz and Mrs. Roopy and Ms. Hannah and all our regular teachers!

"Yay!" we all yelled. "You came back!"

"Klutz!" shouted Dr. Carbles. "I should have *known* it was you! Where have you been all day?"

"We were at Starbucks," said Mr. Klutz. "We decided to chip in and buy our own coffee machine. Now we're ready to get back to work doing what we love—teaching the youth of America."

"Yay!" we all yelled again.

"You can't come back to work, Klutz!" shouted Dr. Carbles. "You're fired! Nick, please escort these students back into the school."

Everybody looked at Mr. Nick.

"Nah, I don't think so, man," said Mr. Nick. "We know when we're not wanted. These kids don't appreciate us. This place is a bummer anyway."

"Where do you think you're going?"

asked Dr. Carbles.

"Let's go to Starbucks," replied Mr. Nick as he got back on the bus.

"You can't leave!" shouted Dr. Carbles. "I hired you for the whole week. You're under contract!"

"We're splittin', dude," said Mr. Nick. "This school gives off bad vibes. Come on, Moon. Let's go get some coffee. Then we'll go back to the yurt."

Mr. Nick's girlfriend, dentist, yoga instructor, and cook got on the bus.

"Wait! Stop! Come back here this minute!" shouted Dr. Carbles. "That's an order!"

"Hey, I don't take orders from The Man,"

said Mr. Nick. "I think for myself." And then he flashed a peace sign at Dr. Carbles as the bus pulled away.

Well, I *think* it was a peace sign. I didn't get a good look at it. Like I said before, I was hungry.

"Who's going to run the school *now*?" asked Andrea.

"Yeah," said Emily. "Who's going to teach us?"

"Klutz!" shouted Dr. Carbles. "You're hired again!"

"Hooray!" we all yelled.

Everybody gathered around Mr. Klutz and our teachers, and we had a big group hug.

"We missed you!"

"We missed you too!"

And we all went back into the school.*

---

*Aren't happy endings nice?

* * *

Well, that's pretty much what happened. Maybe our teachers will be normal again now that they have a coffee machine. Maybe Mr. Cooper will stop tripping over umbrellas. Maybe Mr. Nick will open up a vegetarian bookstore. Maybe Miss Moon will stop playing that horrible love song on her guitar. Maybe Mr. Bob will go back to being a dentist. Maybe Miss Julia will cook something for lunch besides water soup. Maybe we'll have a big dog-washing party. Maybe some porpoises will show up in the all-porpoise room. Maybe Dr. Carbles will go back to Rent-A-Tank. Maybe we'll be able to prevent an asteroid from crashing into the earth and wiping out all life on our planet.

But it won't be easy!

the
eNd

Courtesy of Dan Gutman and Jim Paillot

Dan Gutman

has written many weird books for kids. He lives with his weird wife in New York (a very weird place).

Jim Paillot

lives in Arizona (another weird place) with his weird wife and two weird children. Isn't that weird?